A New True Book

ZEBRAS

By Emilie U. Lepthien

CHILDRENS PRESS®

CHICAGO

Zebras are like horses with stripes.

PHOTO CREDITS
© Erwin & Peggy Bauer–32 (right), 35
© Reinhard Brucker–20
© Virginia R. Grimes–27 (top)
Lauré Communications–© Jason Lauré, 13
North Wind Picture Archives–45 (left)
© Ann Purcell–2
© Carl Purcell–42
Root Resources–© Russel Kriete, 4
Tom Stack & Associates–© Leonard Lee Rue III, 9; © Barbara von Hoffmann, 14 (left), 23; © Larry Tackett, 24; © Joe McDonald, 33
Tony Stone Images–© Johan Elzenga, 6 (bottom); © Jeanne Drake, 21, 27 (bottom); © Chris Harvey, 30; © Doris De Witt, 32 (left)
SuperStock International, Inc.–6 (top left); © AGE FotoStock, 6 (top right); © D.C. Lowe, 10
Valan–© Kennon Cooke, 8, 16, 18 (left); © James D. Markou, 11, 25, 41, 45 (right); © B. Lyon, 13; © S.J. Krasemann, 18 (right), 28, 39
Visuals Unlimited–© Bill Kamin, Cover; © Walt Anderson, 12; © Will Troyer, 14 (right), 37
COVER: Plains zebras

Project Editor: Fran Dyra
Design: Margrit Fiddle

Library of Congress Cataloging-in-Publication Data

Lepthien, Emilie U. (Emilie Utteg)
    Zebras / by Emilie U. Lepthien.
        p.   cm.–(A New true book)
    Includes index.
    ISBN 0-516-01072-7
    1. Zebras–Juvenile literature.   [1.   Zebras.]
I. Title.
QL737.U62L46   1994
599.72'5–dc20
                                          94-10945
                                          CIP
                                          AC

TABLE OF CONTENTS

HORSES WITH STRIPES?

Zebras look like horses with black-and-white stripes. They live in eastern and southern Africa.

Ancient Roman and Greek sailors brought zebras back from Africa almost two thousand years ago. The Romans trained zebras for their circuses. The Greeks called them "horse tigers."

5

Horses (above), donkeys (right), and zebras (below) are all members of the horse family.

Zebras belong to the horse family–Equidae. This family also includes wild asses and donkeys.

ZEBRA SPECIES

There are three species of zebras–Grévy's zebra, the mountain zebra, and the plains zebra. Each species has a different stripe pattern. They also differ in size and in the shape of the head and ears.

Grévy's zebras are the largest. They stand about 5 feet (1.5 meters) high at the shoulder. They have

Grévy's zebras

narrow black stripes, a
white belly, and large,
rounded ears. They live in
Somalia, Ethiopia, and
8 northern Kenya.

The Cape mountain zebra is the smallest zebra.

There are two kinds of mountain zebras. Cape mountain zebras are the smallest. They stand only 4 feet (1.2 meters) tall at the shoulder. They have a small flap of skin called a dewlap under their neck.

9

Hartmann's zebras are threatened by humans. Their migrations are limited by miles of fencing set up by humans to protect their livestock.

Hartmann's zebra is the other mountain zebra. It is slightly larger than the Cape mountain zebra. Fewer than 5,000 of these animals are living today. Both species of mountain zebras are threatened with extinction.

The plains zebra is also called Burchell's zebra.

The plains zebras are the most common species. They live in the grassy woodlands and open plains of East Africa.

Plains zebras stand about 4½ feet (1.4 meters)

A plains zebra (in front) with a Grévy's zebra

tall and weigh from 500 to 600 pounds (227 to 272 kilograms). They have broader stripes and larger hooves than Grévy's zebras.

Not all zebras have black-and-white stripes. The animal in the center has brownish stripes. And young zebras (inset) have brown-and-tan stripes.

SPECIAL STRIPES

Most zebras have black-and-white stripes. But some have brown, gray, yellow, red, or buff-colored stripes. The color depends on the time of year, the area, and the age of the zebra. **13**

Grévy's zebras (left)
have narrow stripes. This plains
zebra (below) has lighter
"shadow" stripes between
the black ones.

In some species, the
stripes are farther apart
with a "shadow" stripe in
between. Others have
narrow stripes set close
together.

14

Some zebras have stripes over their whole body right down to their hooves. Other species have no stripes on their belly or their legs.

Perhaps the most interesting fact about zebras' stripes is that no two animals are exactly alike. Their stripes are like our fingerprints. Just as no two people have the same fingerprints, no two zebras have identical stripe patterns.

STIFF MANES AND
TASSELED TAILS

Like horses, zebras have
a mane–thick hair that grows
on top of the animal's

head and along the back of its neck. The stiff hair on a zebra's mane is striped like its body and stands up straight.

Plains zebras have a long tassel, or tuft of hair, on the tip of their tail. The tail of a mountain zebra ends in a short tuft. Grévy's zebras have a longer tail.

Zebras can turn their ears to catch sounds coming from in front (left) and behind (right).

SPECIAL SENSES

Zebras have a keen sense of hearing. They can turn their ears in different directions to

18

catch the faintest sound.

Zebras also have excellent eyesight. Their eyes are high on the sides of their head. They can see an enemy creeping up even when they are bending down to eat.

Their sharp sense of smell enables zebras to tell friend from foe. It also helps mothers identify their young.

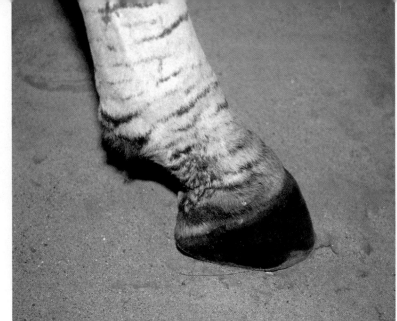

The zebra's hard hoof is small and narrow. Zebras can run over rocky ground better than other animals.

RUNNING

Members of the Equidae family are fast, graceful runners. The third, or middle, toe on each foot is surrounded by a hard hoof. The other toes have disappeared over millions of years.

Zebras have long, slender legs like horses. They have three different speeds, or gaits. In each gait, the legs move in a different way. From slowest

Zebras are fast runners. They can outrun most predators.

to fastest, the gaits are called walk, trot, and gallop. A galloping zebra can reach speeds of 37 miles (60 kilometers) per hour.

Zebras communicate by the position of their ears. A kind of bark warns of danger. They also grunt, whistle, and snort.

A plains zebra grazing on grass in Tanzania

GRAZING ANIMALS

Zebras eat mainly grasses and other small plants. Sometimes they dig for roots. Their diet is low in protein, so they must eat large amounts of food to get the nutrients they need.

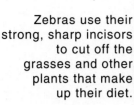
Zebras use their strong, sharp incisors to cut off the grasses and other plants that make up their diet.

Zebras use their soft, flexible lips to gather food. They have sharp front teeth—incisors—on both the upper and lower jaws. They use these teeth to bite off food.

Their strong back teeth—molars—grind up the food. The molars continue growing throughout the animals' lives, so they always have a good grinding surface.

Zebras need large amounts of water. Sometimes they dig holes with their front hooves to find water.

Zebras drinking at a water hole

GROOMING

Zebras like to groom each other. They use their tongue and teeth to clean their coats of dirt and insects. They flick their tail like a flyswatter to brush away insect pests.

Zebras also take dust baths to rid themselves of insects, loose hair, and dry bits of skin. The thin layer of dust that stays on their bodies helps protect them from the blazing sun and biting insects.

Zebras like to roll in the dust. These dust baths help them fight heat and insects.

Oxpeckers hitching a ride on a grazing zebra

Small birds called oxpeckers ride on zebras' backs. Oxpeckers eat the ticks that burrow under the animals' skin. They also warn the zebras of danger by flying away when an enemy comes near.

HERDS AND FAMILIES

Zebras live in herds of 15,000 to 100,000 animals. Every zebra herd has a home range. Ranges may cover 100 to 150 square miles (259 to 388 square kilometers). The herd may migrate 50 to 150 miles (80 to 241 kilometers) to find good grazing land.

The herds are made up of small groups, or families. Like horses, male zebras are called stallions, females are mares, and young zebras are foals.

A family consists of a head stallion and up to six mares and their foals. The mares mate only with the head stallion.

Sometimes the stallions in a herd fight each other for the right to make a

Opposite page:
A zebra herd seen from an airplane in Chobe National Park in the African country of Botswana

Stallions fighting for
control of a zebra family

female part of their family.
   While the herd is on the
move, the stallion protects
his family from predators.
He travels behind his
family. The oldest mare
leads the family when the
stallion is in the rear.

FOALS ARE BORN

Most foals are born in January or February. The stallion stands nearby during the birth to protect the mare and the foal.

A mare and her foal. Most female zebras have one foal.

A newborn foal weighs from 60 to 70 pounds (27 to 32 kilograms) and stands about 3 feet (1 meter) high. Its stripes are brown and tan.

The mare licks her baby's nose, eyes, and ears. This helps form a bond between them. A foal can stand up about 10 minutes after birth. It can walk in half an hour, and in an hour it can run.

A nursing foal

A foal begins drinking
mother's milk when it is
one hour old. Foals live on
their mother's milk for about
seven months. Gradually,
they learn to eat grasses. **35**

Most foals stay with their mother until they are a year old, but some stay longer. Young foals leave when they are old enough to start their own families. Unless they are killed by hunters or predators, zebras may live for 15 to 20 years.

When a stallion dies, the mares and foals stay together and another stallion takes over the family.

This wounded zebra escaped with
its life from a lion attack.

SPECIAL ADAPTATIONS AID SURVIVAL

Zebras are fierce fighters. They have special adaptations that help them survive. Lions, leopards, hyenas, jackals, and wild dogs are their chief animal enemies. The zebra's keen senses warn when predators are near.

When a predator closes in, the zebra fights for its life. A well-placed kick with its hind feet can kill an enemy attacking from behind.

Since their front legs are weaker than their hind legs, zebras do not use them to fight. When attacked from the front or side, they bite with their sharp teeth.

The zebra's stripes make it hard for an enemy to pick out a single zebra.

PROTECTIVE COLORATION

When zebras stand alone,
they are easy to see. But
in a herd the stripes
confuse their enemies.

Zebras escape predators by running very close together. Predators find it hard to pick out an individual zebra to attack. Zebras also use their great speed to outrun a predator.

When two zebras stand together, they face in opposite directions. They can see predators more easily that way.

Zebras on the lookout for predators

If a zebra is too old, too young, or too weak to keep up with the herd, it can become easy prey. Usually the herd slows down to allow a slower animal to catch up.

A herd of zebras migrating to find a good supply of food and water

PROBLEMS

Humans are the greatest enemies of zebras. Poachers hunt the animals illegally for their hides and tails. Poachers often attack at night along a migration trail or at a water hole.

42

Farmers are taking over the land that zebras use for grazing. The areas where zebras can live are shrinking every day.

Zebras are also plagued with diseases and parasites. Flies are bothersome. Blood-sucking ticks and other insects burrow into their hides. And anthrax—a fatal disease—infects zebras.

EXTINCTION IS FOREVER

Hunting can lead to the extinction of a species. The most beautiful zebra of all–the quagga–died out in 1883. The quagga lived in southern Africa. Its name came from its barking call–"kwa-ha."

Early colonists killed quaggas for their meat and hides. Their coats were striking, with alternating dark brown and white stripes. Their legs, undersides, rear half, and long, flowing tail

The quagga (left) was hunted to extinction in the nineteenth century. The remaining zebra species must be protected if they are to survive.

had no stripes. These beautiful animals were slaughtered mercilessly. The last quagga died in a zoo in Europe in 1883.

If illegal poaching continues, other zebra species could go the way of the quagga.

45

WORDS YOU SHOULD KNOW

adaptation (ah • dap • TAY • shun)—the act of changing to fit new living conditions

anthrax (AN • thrax)—a fatal disease that infects horses, zebras, cattle, sheep, etc.

dewlap (DOO • lap)—a flap of skin that hangs down under an animal's neck

Equidae (EK • wih • day)—the animal family that includes horses, zebras, wild asses, and donkeys

extinction (ex • TINK • shun)—the dying out of a species of plant or animal

fingerprints (FING • ger • prints)—the marks left on smooth surfaces by a person's fingers

flexible (FLEX • ih • bil)—easily bent

foal (FOLE)—a young horse or zebra

grazing (GRAY • zing)—eating grasses and other small plants

identical (eye • DEN • tih • kil)—the same in every way; exactly alike

incisors (in • SYE • zerz)—long, sharp front teeth

migrate (MY • grait)—to travel, usually for a long distance, to find better food or better weather conditions

molars (MOH • lerz)—broad, flat back teeth

nutrients (NOO • tree • ints)—elements that are essential to keep living things strong and healthy, such as proteins, carbohydrates, fats, vitamins, and minerals

oxpecker (AHX • peck • er)—a small bird that rides on the backs of large animals and feeds on parasites

parasites (PAIR • uh • sytes)—animals that live on or inside larger animals

poachers (POH • cherz)—people who kill animals illegally

predator (PREH • dih • ter)—an animal that kills and eats other animals

protective coloration (pro • TEK • tiv kul • er • AY • shun)–a pattern of colors and markings that makes an animal hard to see

protein (PROH • teen)–a substance in food that animals need to be healthy

quagga (KWAG • ah)–an extinct zebra species

range (RAINJ)–the region in which a plant or animal can be found in the wild

species (SPEE • seez)–a group of related plants or animals that are able to interbreed

stallion (STAL • yun)–a male horse or zebra

tick (TIK)–a small, eight-legged insect that looks like a spider and burrows into the skin of a larger animal

INDEX

About the Author

Emilie U. Lepthien received her BA and MS degrees and certificate in school administration from Northwestern University. She taught upper-grade science and social studies, wrote and narrated science programs for the Chicago Public Schools' station WBEZ, and was principal in Chicago, Illinois, for twenty years. She received the American Educator's Medal from Freedoms Foundation.

She is a member of Delta Kappa Gamma Society International, Chicago Principals' Association, Illinois Women's Press Association, National Federation of Press Women, and AAUW.

She has written books in the Enchantment of the World, New True Books, and America the Beautiful series.